W9-DFQ-836

É

Amyle

The Mystery of the Golden Pearls

A Halloween Adventure in Clarkesville

Amadeus
The Traveling Dog

Published and distributed by

Legacy Publishers

division of Evaluation Enterprises, Inc.
2386 Clower Street, Building G, Suite 101
Snellville, GA 30078-6134
Information and Orders: 1.800.290.8055 or 770.979.7899
E-mail: Legacy@eeinc.org
http://www.eeinc.org

Printed in China
ISBN 1-932957-02-2

First Printing

This book is dedicated to all the Ghosts and Goblins who come to Clarkesville, GA for a wonderful Halloween adventure!

3

My name is Amadeus. You say it like this: "Ah-muh-day-us."
I am a Great Pyrenees Mountain Dog.
I am a Certified Canine Good Citizen with the American Kennel Club.

Please visit my website at
http://www.eeinc.org/amadeus/
amadeusbooks.com

4

This books belongs to:

Vestavia Hills Library

This is my right, front paw.
(I have fluffy white fur between my toes).

Amadeus
The Traveling Dog

It was the night before Halloween.
There was a chill in the crisp, mountain air.
The full moon was bright orange,
  like a big, round, perfect pumpkin hanging in the darkness.
Stars were shining,
  as bright as new pennies.
You could hear the sounds of night all around.
It was a perfect night for a Halloween mystery.

Clarkesville was getting ready for the Halloween Festival.
Children and adults would wear costumes.
The stores would give out candy and prizes.
The Halloween Princess would be crowned.
She would wear a special crown,
  a crown with a circle of Golden Pearls right in the center.

In the nearby woods,
Creepy Coyote crept through the trees.
He hoped that no one saw him.
He had a secret plan to spoil Halloween.
He did not want the Halloween
    Princess to be crowned.

"Ooowww! Ooowww!
    Hello Moon," he howled.
"Light my way
    through the dark woods."

"There will be no Halloween fun in Clarkesville tomorrow night,"
    he muttered to himself.
Creepy Coyote did not like Halloween.
On Halloween night people walk through the woods,
    and he cannot go hunting for food.
Coyotes are shy and hunt mostly at night.

"Besides," he thought, "People hate coyotes.
No one ever wears a coyote costume on Halloween."

The princess had left her crown on the small porch.
Creepy Coyote waited for his chance.
He saw the Halloween Princess go into the kitchen
    to help her mother with dinner.
He sneaked onto the porch.
He grabbed the circle of Golden Pearls from the crown.
Then the thief disappeared into the night.

On the morning of Halloween, I was riding through the mountains
   to look at the pretty fall leaves.
Some leaves were red.
Some leaves were orange.
Some leaves were gold, just like the Golden Pearls.

Three nice ladies in Dillard told me about
   the Halloween Festival in the town of Clarkesville.

The town of Clarkesville was buzzing
   with activity.
People were talking about the
   stolen jewels.
"We must find the Golden Pearls soon,"
   they were saying.
"The Halloween Princess cannot wear
   her crown without the Golden Pearls."

"That Creepy Coyote is a thief," said Spider Man.
"The sheriff has searched everywhere,
   but the Golden Pearls have not been found.
The Halloween Princess will be very sad.
There will be no Golden Pearls in her crown tonight."

"Amadeus, will you help find the Golden Pearls?" asked a small, brown, fuzzy dog.

"Woof, woof," I said. "I will do what I can to help."
He smiled and said, "Thank you."

Where would I start?
I kept my eyes and ears open, looking and listening for clues.

13

Lovely Lioness was very helpful.
"Maybe Creepy Coyote has gone to
  Tallulah Gorge State Park," she said.
"There are lots of woods and rivers
  and waterfalls at the park."
That sounded like a clue to me.

14

"Tallulah Gorge State Park has nice walking trails," said Bewitching Witch. "It is a very large park. A coyote could hide out there." I knew what my next move would be.

Inside the park, paths were made of recycled rubber tires.
They felt good under my tired feet.

"Let me give you a hug for good luck, Amadeus," said Ruth. "Go and find the Golden Pearls that the coyote has hidden."

I climbed on top of a high rock to look for clues.
I smelled coyote tracks.
I began to follow the tracks.

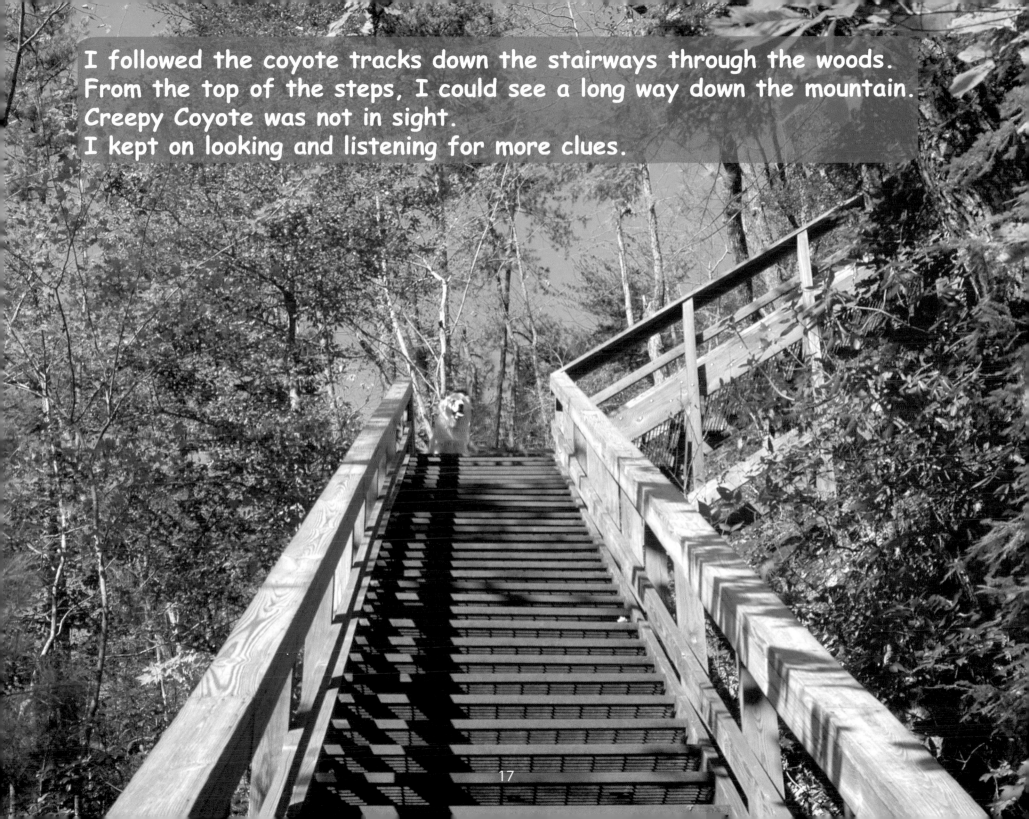

I followed the coyote tracks down the stairways through the woods.
From the top of the steps, I could see a long way down the mountain.
Creepy Coyote was not in sight.
I kept on looking and listening for more clues.

The tracks led to a long,
   wooden, swinging bridge.
It looked scary,
   but I was brave.

As I hurried across, I
   looked along the banks
   of the river far below.

Still no coyote.

The coyote tracks stopped at the waterfall.
"He was here," said Sammy Squirrel. "The best clue is in the water.
That's what I heard Creepy Coyote say to his coyote friends.
Go to the Potter's Mark.
Mr. Limpet the trout lives in the river there. He can help you."
Sammy Squirrel knew all the animals in the woods. I trusted him.

I took one last look high above the gorge.

I am a big dog. But this cliff is so high that I look very small behind the fence.
I always obey park safety rules and never climb over safety fences.

There was no sign of the Golden Pearls.
The sun was beginning to set.
Time was running out.
I followed Sammy Squirrel's clue.

Mr. Limpet, the trout poked his head out of the water. "Creepy Coyote is jealous of Halloween fun," he said. "He put the Golden Pearls in a place where no person would dare go this time of year. It would be too cold. That's what my trout friends heard him say."

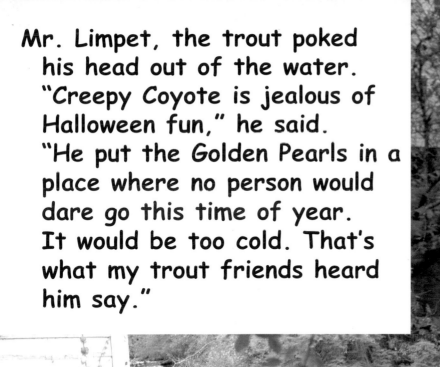

I knew that must be a clue.
It is a riddle clue.
If I can solve the riddle,
    I can find the Golden Pearls.

Riding through the winding mountain roads, I thought about all the clues.

Water is a clue.
Too cold for people is a clue.

I saw a strange rock near the woods. There was a hole under it. Just then a coyote came sneaking out from behind the rock.

This must be Creepy Coyote's den! It was another clue.
The Golden Pearls must be nearby.
I was getting close.
I could feel it in my bones.

Black Rock Lake was at the
   bottom of the hill.
I had a feeling that I might find
   another clue there.
Besides, I was thirsty.
A long drink from a cold mountain
   lake would be great.

BLACK ROCK LAKE
ELEVATION 2241 FT.

Brrrr! The water was very
cold. Miss Mary would not
like to swim in this.

But I am a Great Pyrenees
Mountain dog. I like the
cold water.

I lapped the water with my tongue.
How cool it was!
How good it tasted!
How it sparkled!

Sparkle? Water doesn't sparkle!
It was another clue!

Something was in the water.
It sparkled from the bottom
  of the lake.

The Golden Pearls!

What a surprise!

The Halloween Princess will
be so happy.

24

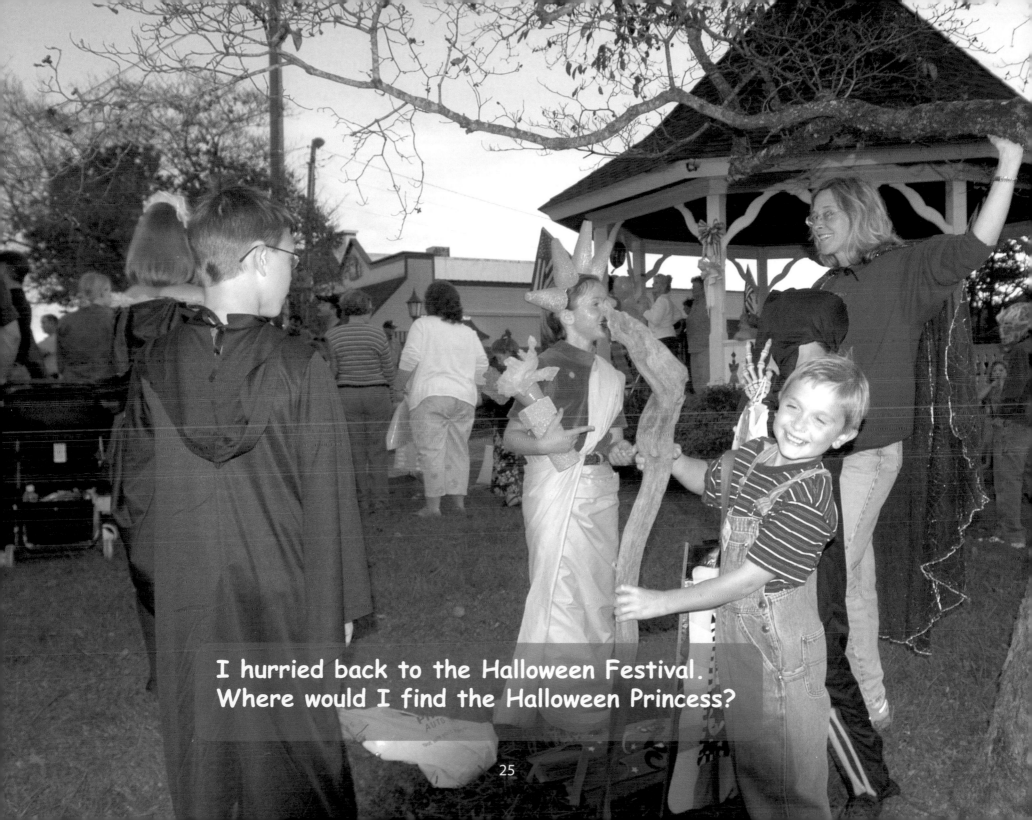

I hurried back to the Halloween Festival. Where would I find the Halloween Princess?

Warrior Queen did not know
where the Halloween Princess was.

Neither did Lady Dracula.

I went on my way.

The twin baby cows said, "Goo goo. Moo moo."
They had not seen the Halloween Princess.

Sunny Sunflower came up to me.
"I am sorry that I cannot help you,
Amadeus," she said.
"I hope you find the
   Halloween Princess in time."

Ghosts and gobblins were everywhere. But no one could find the Halloween Princess.

It was enough to make a person want to scream!

But I kept on looking.

Minnie Mouse did not know where the Halloween Princess was.
But Tooth Fairy did.
"Come with me," she said.
"The Halloween Princess is a friend of mine.
I will take you to her."

"Bless you, Amadeus," said Tooth Fairy. "Finding the Golden Pearls took a lot of courage."

The moment I saw her, I knew she was the Halloween Princess.

She was standing right behind Tooth Fairy.

The Golden Pearls were missing from her crown.

33

The Halloween Princess was happy to see the Golden Pearls.

The pearls were placed on her crown, right in front where they belonged. There was a matching set of Golden Pearls on her princess robe.

I bowed to the Halloween Princess. She was very kind and beautiful.

The Halloween Princess invited me to stay for the Halloween Festival.

It was the best Halloween ever!

I will be back in Clarkesville next year for another Halloween adventure.

I hope to see you there!

The End